T0198838

We Eat Rainbows!

Cynthia Myers-Morrison EdD
with
Annica Strandberg-Schmidt,
Bitten Jonsson, Esther-Helga
Gudmundsdottir, Judy Wolfe,
Katra Lesjak, Rachel Murray,
and Dr. Vera Tarman

To order additional copies of this book, contact:
Xlibris
844-714-8691
www.Xlibris.com
Orders@Xlibris.com

ISBN: Softcover   979-8-3694-0355-6
            EBook   979-8-3694-0354-9

Print information available on the last page

Rev. date: 07/29/2023

We Eat
Rainbows!

Dedication

Dr. Vera Tarman for the inspiration for this book for children and those who care about them.

The "WE" in this book includes Every Child, Every Adolescent, and Every Adult of whatever age and especially those who show kindness, respect, love, and care for each person and for the animals we love.

We ALL strive to eat Rainbows! We eat real foods that are rainbow colors.

Be kind to yourself and others.

Choose wisely. Our choices make a difference for our bodies and brains. Our animal friends will show us food choices and some "Life Between Meals" choices. Choose wisely.

We spend our time in activities of buying food, cooking, playing, working, and resting.

May you never crave anything! (If you are craving, it may be something that does not suit you.) One day at a time.

Our animal friends say, "EAT VIOLET/INDIGO!" Beets, eggplants, purple cabbages, plums, and blackberries.

We cook together AS A FAMILY and enjoy cooking healthy whole foods, eating together, sitting in a forest campsite.

We enjoy brown bag lunches, national and city parks, walking, hiking, bicycling, swimming, other outdoor activities, leaving a smaller footprint on the planet by carrying away anything carried into a natural area, and then recycling all we can at home.

Our animal friends say, "EAT BLUE!" Boysenberries, blueberries, and blackberries. (In this picture, what is NOT blue?)

We enjoy buying local, seasonal produce at roadside stands or community-sponsored agriculture sites. Do you have a CSA near you? Do you see roadside stands when you are riding your bicycles?

Our animal friends say, "EAT GREEN!" Edamame, kale, pickles, cucumbers, asparagus, celery, green peppers, artichokes, chard, Brussel sprouts, zucchini, leaves of all kinds, spinach, broccoli, sprouts, watercress, broccoli rabe, fennel, kohlrabi, okra, parsley, green peppers, chilies, jalapenos, green beans, tomatillos, seaweed, avocados, green cabbage, honeydew, kiwi, limes, and pears.

We are shopping at the grocery store with all these yellow foods available. Is the fruit and vegetable section your favorite part of the market?

Our animal friends say, "EAT YELLOW!" Spaghetti squash, crookneck squash, yellow pepper, rutabaga, summer squash, butternut squash, yellow carrots, mango, melon, nectarines, pineapple, grapefruit, lemon, and casaba melon.

With the Burmese cats playing in a backyard garden, we are working together near a fruit tree orchard. We prepare the earth, plant, trim, weed, water, and harvest while our cats play.

Our animal friends say, "EAT ORANGE!" Carrots, squashes, pumpkin, orange peppers, acorn squash, peaches, apricots, cantaloupe, oranges, and tangerines.

With the cats on the lookout for a nibble or two, we enjoy sharing healthy food that we prepare and eat with others. Do you wonder why we are laughing? Usually, the laughter comes from the daily stories we share.

On the table in front of us is an abundance of fruit and vegetables newly harvested from the garden, brought home from the local market, or purchased at a farmers' market.

Our animal friends say, "EAT RED!" Red peppers, radishes, tomatoes, pimiento, red cabbage, strawberries, raspberries, apples, cranberries, pomegranates, pink grapefruit, and rhubarb.

The calico cat encourages us to enjoy colorful herbs and spices weekly. Try out new ones. Cinnamon, nutmeg, turmeric, curry, Himalayan pink sea salt, black pepper, red pepper, garlic, real salt, oregano, rosemary, thyme, basil, cardamom, tarragon, ginger, and more!

Our animal friends say, "EAT WHITE!" Ginger, mushrooms, white asparagus, mushrooms, parsnips, turnips, cabbage, cauliflower, jicama, garlic, leeks, onions, sauerkraut, scallions, shallots, and bananas.

Dairy

We work in the garden to harvest, hoe, and carry the abundant produce to a waiting place to clean and prepare it for eating. The dairy cows and goat notice the people.

Our animal friends say, "Eat Dairy!" (except for those who experience tummy problems, a rash, wheezing, or another allergic response. This exception applies to any food that gives you those experiences or creates cravings.) Goat milk, sheep milk, cow milk, cheese, kefir milk, yogurt, cottage cheese, and ricotta.

Eat proteins and fats!

Proteins can be as varied as eggs, shrimp, squid, buffalo, bison, all wild game, salmon, mackerel, sardines, turkey, beef, crab, clams, cod, mussels, oysters, tuna, trout, sole, tilapia, lobster, whitefish, pork, chicken, turkey, scallops, lamb, tofu, and soy.

Fats: Avocados, chia and flaxseeds, grass-fed butter, coconut oil, olive oil, walnuts, whole milk and yogurt from grass-fed cows, wild-caught fish, especially fatty cold-water fish (like salmon, trout, sardines, and herring), cheese, and olives.

We play beside springs, streams, lakes, and oceans. We may have to purify water if we drink from these bodies of water; however, when we bring refillable containers of water from home, usually that water has already been purified and treated to allow us to drink it without further purification.

Have you and your family visited a water purification plant to see the processes that prepare our water to be drinkable?

Are you aware of how many young people in the world must carry water from distant locations to their families' homes to have drinking water and water with which to cook and clean? Have you ever carried a bucket or jug of water? Do you know how heavy it is?

Our animal friends say, "Drink WATER!" Enjoy water. Take your weight in pounds and divide it by 2, and drink daily that number of ounces in water. You can add lemon or lime juice to the water. If you are thirsty, you have waited too long to drink the water! Do you have a container with ounces marked on it? Use it to see the quantity you may need to drink daily.

Avoid drinking sugary sweetened beverages.

RESEARCH

Research the vitamins, minerals, and antioxidants in each color and food you eat. What are the proteins, fats, and carbohydrates in these foods?

What other foods do you and your family eat?

Research them to identify your healthiest choices: nuts, beans, lentils, grains, starches, prosciutto, bacon, sausage, sweeteners, and juices.

Choose real foods, preferably with one ingredient listed and no bags or boxes.

Substances to avoid include soda pop, sugar, high fructose corn syrup, trans fats, industrial oils, alcohol, alcohol extracts, caffeine, juices, flours, artificial sweeteners, processed and ultra-processed substances.

CHOOSE VARIETY!

Try out new foods and herbs and spices each week.

What kinds of exercise work best for you and your family members?

How many hours of sleep are best for you and each of your family members? Are you all asleep between 10 pm and 2 am?

Do you go outside to see the sunrise and go somewhere to see the sunset daily? Do you journal and include the physical, mental, and emotional responses you have after what you eat and drink?

Growing food, shopping for food, cooking and preparing food, setting the table, clearing the dishes, and washing/drying dishes are all things we can participate in doing in our food-related lives.

Some recipes follow. Enjoy cooking with family members. Then enjoy eating your creativity!

Quick and Easy Salmon Cakes

4 servings
25 minutes

Ingredients

12 ozs Canned Wild Salmon
3 tbsps Extra Virgin Olive Oil
6 Egg (Yolks only)
1 Sweet Onion (small)
Lemon
1 tsp Chives
2 tsps Parsley
Sea Salt & Black Pepper (to taste)

Nutrition

Amount per serving	
Calories	359
Fat	22g
Carbs	7g
Fiber	1g
Sugar	4g
Protein	32g
Sodium	441mg
Potassium	471mg
Vitamin A	629IU
Vitamin C	5mg
Calcium	91mg
Iron	2mg
Vitamin D	792IU
Vitamin E	4mg
Vitamin B6	0.3mg
Folate	59µg
Vitamin B12	5.4µg
Magnesium	37mg
Zinc	2mg
Selenium	53µg

Directions

1   Preheat the oven to bake at 350 degrees. Line a baking sheet with parchment paper.

2   In a large mixing bowl, combine the salmon, egg yolks. Add in the minced onion, and stir to combine all ingredients.

3   Using your hands, form the salmon mixture into 2 ounce patties, and place each cake on the parchment lined baking sheet. Bake salmon cakes for 15 minutes.

4   Remove the cakes from the oven, and heat oil in a cast iron skillet over medium high heat. Fry the cakes for about a minute on either side, or until they are golden brown and crispy on the outside.

5   Serve with a squeeze of lemon, some minced chives, salt, pepper and parsley.

Zucchini Boat Pizza

1 serving
45 minutes

Ingredients

1 Zucchini (medium)

4 ozs Pork Sausage

1/2 Garlic (cloves, minced)

1/4 tsp Italian Seasoning

3 tbsps Tomato Sauce

2 ozs Mozzarella Cheese (grated)

2 tbsps Mushrooms (thinly sliced)

1/16 Green Bell Pepper (chopped)

1 1/2 tsps Red Onion (chopped)

1 tbsp Green Olives (sliced)

Nutrition

Amount per serving	
Calories	567
Fat	44g
Carbs	13g
Fiber	3g
Sugar	7g
Protein	27g
Sodium	1298mg
Potassium	916mg
Vitamin A	1136IU
Vitamin C	45mg
Calcium	266mg
Iron	3mg
Vitamin D	51IU
Vitamin E	1mg
Vitamin B6	0.6mg
Folate	57µg
Vitamin B12	0.7µg
Magnesium	60mg
Zinc	2mg
Selenium	2µg

Directions

1 Preheat the oven to 375°F (190°C) and line a baking sheet with parchment paper.

2 Scoop the seeds out of the zucchini and discard. Place the zucchini on the prepared baking sheet cut side up.

3 In a pan over medium-high heat brown the sausage. Add the garlic and Italian seasoning and cook for another minute. Add the tomato sauce and stir to combine.

4 Sliced the sausages into 1/4" slices. Divide the sausage slices between the scooped out zucchini. Top with cheese, mushrooms, bell pepper, onions and olives. Bake for 23 to 25 minutes or until the cheese has melted and the zucchini is tender. Divide between plates and enjoy!

Notes

Leftovers: Refrigerate in an airtight container for up to three days.

Serving Size: One serving is two zucchini boats.

Dairy-Free: Use a dairy-free cheese.

More Flavor: Use mild Italian or spicy sausages.

No Pork Sausage: Use chicken or turkey sausages instead.

Cauliflower & Egg Breakfast Muffins

6 servings
25 minutes

Ingredients

4 ozs Prosciutto (roughly chopped)
5 cups Cauliflower Rice
4 Egg
1 cup Arugula (roughly chopped)
1/4 cup Parsley (finely chopped)
1/2 cup Nutritional Yeast
Sea Salt & Black Pepper (to taste)

Nutrition

Amount per serving	
Calories	152
Fat	6g
Carbs	8g
Fiber	5g
Sugar	2g
Protein	17g
Sodium	450mg
Potassium	461mg
Vitamin A	473IU
Vitamin C	4mg
Calcium	50mg
Iron	2mg
Vitamin D	27IU
Vitamin E	0mg
Vitamin B6	10.2mg
Folate	23µg
Vitamin B12	45.3µg
Magnesium	7mg
Zinc	0mg
Selenium	10µg

Directions

1. Preheat the oven to 375°F (191°C) and lightly grease a muffin tin.

2. Heat a large skillet over medium heat. Add the prosciutto and cook for a 3 minutes per side or until crisp. Remove from the pan and set aside.

3. In a large bowl add the cauliflower rice, eggs, arugula, parsley, nutritional yeast, sea salt and pepper. Mix well to combine.

4. Scoop the cauliflower mix into the muffin tin, filling to the top and creating a small hollow space in the top. Add the prosciutto to the hollowed-out space. Place in the oven and bake for 15 minutes. Remove, let it cool slightly and then serve and enjoy!

Notes

Leftovers: Refrigerate in an airtight container for up to three days. Freeze for up to two months.

Serving Size: One serving is equal to two cauliflower egg bites.

More Flavor: Use parmesan or pecorino instead of nutritional yeast. Add chili flakes to the mix.

No Arugula: Use spinach.

WE EAT RAINBOWS!

Eat Rainbows each week and daily when possible. Use this chart to compare what you eat with what each family member eats. Can everyone in the family eat a rainbow? Each week? And then, each day?

Instructions: Copy one chart for each family member. Write the servings/portions of the foods, color, proteins, fats, water, spices, and hours of sleep and exercise and sunrises and sunsets.

	Monday	Tuesday	Wednesday	Thursday	Friday	Saturday	Sunday
Violet/Indigo							
Blue							
Green							
Yellow							
Orange							
Red							
White							
Proteins							
Fats							
Water							
Spices							
Sleep							
Exercise							
Sunrise							
Sunset							

WE EAT RAINBOWS!

Enjoy VARIETY!

We Eat a Rainbow each week and then we strive to Eat a Rainbow each day. Then we attempt to encourage everyone to Eat a Rainbow every day with real food prepared at home and eaten with family and friends while in conversation sharing experiences. We share about sunrises and sunsets, school, work, play, and something learned each day by each person at the table. Conversation and support grow. Our meals become shared JOYS!

	Monday	Tuesday	Wednesday	Thursday	Friday	Saturday	Sunday
Violet/Indigo							
Blue							
Green							
Yellow							
Orange							
Red							
White							
Proteins							
Fats							
Water							
Spices							
Sleep							
Exercise							
Sunrise							
Sunset							

WE EAT RAINBOWS! JOURNAL

You may choose to journal and include the responses you have after what you eat and drink. Have you kept track of what, where, and how much you eat? Doing this occasionally (or every day if you like) can help to encourage awareness and variety!

_____
_____
_____
_____
_____
_____
_____
_____
_____
_____
_____
_____
_____
_____
_____
_____
_____
_____
_____
_____
_____
_____
_____

WE EAT RAINBOWS! JOURNAL

What are the responses felt immediately or one or two hours after eating and four or five hours later? For example, if you are very, very hungry one to two hours after eating a meal, you may not be eating enough real food at your meal. To be hungry so soon may also mean it is a craving, and you are eating something that is an allergen for you. You might be itching or sniffling or licking your lips or getting sleepy or angry or something else. You might break out in a rash or start to wheeze or cough. If any of these things happen, ask for help because it could be serious. Notice how you feel four or five hours after the end of your previous meal of the day. Do you notice that it is time to eat? What differences do you notice between the feeling after a couple of hours and the feeling after four or five hours? The first may be a craving, and the second probably is hunger. Hunger experienced when it has been several hours since eating is an appropriate response. Cravings are avoidable if we choose healthy, real food in appropriate quantities for our ages and activity levels. Choose wisely.

_____

_____

_____

_____

_____

_____

_____

_____

_____

_____

_____

_____

_____

_____

_____

_____

We Eat Rainbows!

Our Animal Friends

Can you identify the animals in the book? (The answers are on the back cover.) Each one encouraged us to eat a color of the rainbow. Which animal encouraged which color? Look carefully at the color of the collar for a clue.

Do you know there are two ways to remember the rainbow colors in order? One is VIBGYOR and the other is ROY G BIV. Which do you prefer? Which are used in this book and where?

Printed in the United States
by Baker & Taylor Publisher Services